This Walker book belongs to:

. . . .

. . . .

. . . .

The World CHAMPION

First published 2011 by Walker Books Ltd
87 Vauxhall Walk, London SE11 5HJ

This edition published 2012

10 9 8 7 6 5 4 3 2 1

Text © 2011 Sean Taylor
Illustrations © 2011 Jimmy Liao

The right of Sean Taylor and Jimmy Liao to be identified as author and illustrator
respectively of this work has been asserted by them in accordance with the
Copyright, Designs and Patents Act 1988

This book has been typeset in Memphis

Printed in China

British Library Cataloguing in Publication Data
a catalogue record for this book is available from the British Library

ISBN 978-1-4063-3834-8

www.walker.co.uk

# of Staying Awake

SEAN TAYLOR

illustrated by **JIMMY LIAO**

WALKER BOOKS
AND SUBSIDIARIES

LONDON • BOSTON • SYDNEY • AUCKLAND

For Christine
~ **S. T.**

For Roro
~ **J. L.**

"Good night, Stella," says Dad.
"Time to go to bed."

But how can Stella go to bed?
She still has Cherry Pig,
Thunderbolt the puppet mouse
and Beanbag Frog to get to sleep.

"I'm a bit wide awake,"
snuffles Cherry Pig.

"I'm a *lot* wide awake!"
calls out Thunderbolt.

And Beanbag Frog is worse than
wide awake. He's going hoppety-hop.

"Stoppety-stop!" says Stella.   "I'm not going to sleep!"
"It's time to go to bed."   calls out Thunderbolt.

"Sleep is too slow!"
croaks Beanbag Frog.

**"I'm the world champion of
staying awake!"** says Cherry Pig.

But Stella is good at thinking
up ways to get them to sleep.

So she puts them on her pillow.
"Can you dream the pillow into
something?" asks Cherry Pig.

"Yes," says Stella.

"It's a ship."

And it is...

The Pillow Ship rocks.
The Pillow Ship sways.
The Pillow Ship sails
across the waves.

In the deep water
under the boat,
jellyfish, sharks and
seahorses float.

But down in the cabin,
you'll come to no harm.
You'll be warm as a cat
sleeping inside a barn.

So snuggle your feet,
snuggle your knees,
and let yourself sway
over the seas.

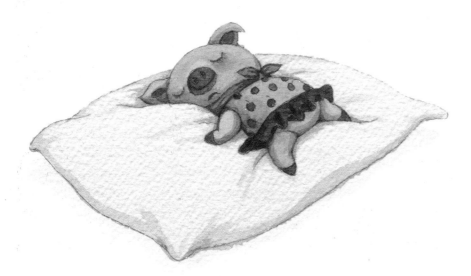

Quietly, Stella checks.

Cherry Pig is asleep.

But Beanbag Frog asks,
"Is jelly made from jellyfish?"

And Thunderbolt is calling out,
"The world champion of staying awake is actually ME!"

"How am I ever going to
get you two to sleep?"
sighs Stella.

"With presents, toys and fireworks
and spicy-sausage pizza?"
suggests Thunderbolt.

"It's not time for anything like that," Stella tells them. "It's time to *shut your eyes*."

"I've shut my eyes, but my feet are completely woken-up," says Beanbag Frog, in a very bouncy voice.

So Stella puts them
in her shoe box.

"Can you dream this box into
something?" asks Thunderbolt.

"Yes," says Stella.

"It's a train."

And it is...

Outside, the air
     is cold with rain,
but it's warm and dry
     on the Midnight Train.

The silver wheels
     spin round on the track
on their way over
     the mountains and back.

And, as it chugs
     and clatters and steams,
the train will carry you
     into your dreams.

Dreams of long journeys
and dinosaur eggs.
Dreams of white horses
with galloping legs.

"Who's the world champion
of staying awake now?"
whispers Stella.

Thunderbolt lifts his head and says,
**"I'm the world champion of ...
going ... to sleep."**

Then he closes his eyes.

So that leaves Beanbag Frog.   Is he asleep?

No. He's not.
He's going
hoppety-hop
again.

"How many years is
it to my birthday?"
he asks Stella.

"I can't believe you're still awake!" she whispers.

"I can!" says his croaky voice. **"The world champion of staying awake must actually be ME!"**

"Yes," says Stella.

So Stella puts him in the toy basket.
"Can you dream our basket into
something?" asks Beanbag Frog.

And it is...

"It's a balloon."

The Star Ship Balloon
flies off and away,
leaving behind
the last of today.

Through air as quiet
as fallen snow,
up and up and up
you go.

Up so high that it's best
  to stop
if you feel like going
  hoppety-hop.

And what's around you
  as you rise?
The sparkling necklaces
  of the skies.

Stella checks. Beanbag Frog is lying with his head on one arm.

Not a croak. Not a bounce. Not a hoppety-hop.

"They're *all* fast asleep," she whispers.

And she tucks them, one by one, into bed.

So the world champion of staying awake
must actually be Stella.

Or perhaps not.

Sean Taylor has written more than twenty books for young children.
He divides his time between the United Kingdom and Brazil.
Look out for his next Walker title, coming soon!

Illustrator **Jimmy Liao**'s books have sold over
five million copies throughout the world. He lives in Taiwan.
Look out for Jimmy's next Walker title coming soon too!

Also illustrated by Jimmy Liao:

ISBN 978-1-4063-1554-7

Available from all good booksellers
www.walker.co.uk